Homes
From Start to Finish

Claire Kreger

Photographs by Patrick Carney

BLACKBIRCH®
PRESS

THOMSON
GALE

San Diego • Detroit • New York • San Francisco • Cleveland • New Haven, Conn. • Waterville, Maine • London • Munich

THOMSON

GALE

For more information, contact
The Gale Group, Inc.
27500 Drake Rd.
Farmington Hills, MI 48331-3535
Or you can visit our Internet site at http://www.gale.com

Photo Credits: Cover, all photos © Patrick Carney except for pages 18, 19, 20, 21 © CORBIS

LIBRARY OF CONGRESS CATALOGING-IN-PUBLICATION DATA

Kreger, Claire, 1973-
  Homes : from start to finish / by Claire Kreger ; photographs by Patrick Carney.
    v. cm. — (Made in the USA)
  Includes bibliographical references and index.
  Contents: The design — Frank Lloyd Wright: Architectural innovator — Clear the area! — Foundation — Building the floor — Raise the walls — Electric and plumbing — The roof — Colonial and Spanish style homes — Windows and doors — Insulation — Drywall — Siding — Finishing up — From a house to a home.
  ISBN 1-4103-0169-9 (hardback : alk. paper)
  1. House construction—Juvenile literature. 2. Dwellings—Juvenile literature. [1. House construction. 2. Dwellings.] I. Carney, Patrick, ill. II. Title. III. Series: Made in the U.S.A.

TH4811.5.K74 2004
690'.8—dc21   2003002016

Contents

Acknowledgments
This book is dedicated to my housemates, Double-A and Zoey G.

Special Thanks
I especially want to thank Breck Barnett and Chapman Construction for their help with this book.

It takes many workers with different jobs to build a home.

Houses line millions of streets in towns all across America. In fact, there are more than 100 million houses in the United States! Though houses look different from each other on the outside, most are built in the same way.

There are many steps that a new house must go through before it is ready to be lived in. Most people hire a contractor to manage the construction project. The contractor is in charge of hiring everyone else who works on the house. These other workers are called subcontractors. Construction workers, plumbers, and electricians are all subcontractors. They must all work very closely with each other to build a new home. But, how is a house actually built?

3

4

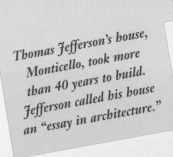

Thomas Jefferson's house, Monticello, took more than 40 years to build. Jefferson called his house an "essay in architecture."

The Design

Before a house can be built, someone has to design it. The person who draws the blueprints, or plans, for a house is called an architect. Everyone who works on building a house uses these blueprints. These drawings show where each room should be, and what size and shape it should be. The architect's plans also show plumbers and electricians where to work.

Architects work very closely with the people who hired them. They discuss their drawings and make changes when needed. The next step after blueprints is for architects to make a computer model of the house. Sometimes, they also build a small 3-D model of the home. They use clay, cardboard, wire, and paint to make the model look as much like the real house as possible. This model will show the client what the house will look like when it is finished. When clients and architects agree on a design, it's time for the next step.

Left: *Each person who works on building a house must follow the blueprints.*

Above: *Blueprints are drawings that show what a house will look like.*

Frank Lloyd Wright: Architectural Innovator

Frank Lloyd Wright was born in Wisconsin in 1867. He was one of the world's most important architects. He created a whole new way to design buildings. Nearly 500 of his designs were built. Wright designed buildings to blend in with the environment. This style was called organic architecture.

His designs called for rooms to have open space. He made changes to American homes such as adding living rooms and carports. He designed many homes and buildings so they would fit naturally into their surroundings.

Though Frank Lloyd Wright mostly designed homes for single families, he also designed churches, museums, bridges, and skyscrapers. In many cities, Wright designed structures that were like sculptures. Perhaps his most famous design is the Guggenheim Museum in New York City. The Guggenheim was built in 1956 to house modern art. Tourists often visit the beautiful building and never make it inside to see the art!

Opposite: The Guggenheim Museum in New York City was built in 1956.
Opposite inset : Architect Frank Lloyd Wright designed more than 500 buildings.

GENHEIM MUSEUM 7

Clear the Area!

The area where a new house is to be built is called a site. A site must be cleared before construction can begin. A site-preparation crew may use a bulldozer or backhoe to cut down trees. They get rid of any rocks or brush that may get in the way. Sometimes this crew is the same group of workers who dig the foundation for the new home.

A construction worker uses a bulldozer to clear a building site.

The Foundation

Most modern houses are built on a foundation. A foundation makes the building site flat. A crew digs a hole at the site. How deep the hole is depends on what type of foundation the client wants. This also determines how much concrete is used. There are three kinds of foundations: basements, crawl spaces, and slabs. Basements are rooms under houses. Crawl spaces raise houses up off the ground. They also create a space where plumbing can go. Slabs are like huge solid concrete floors.

A foundation is built to level a site.

A power drill is one of many tools construction workers use to build the floor.

Building the Floor

Unless the foundation of the house is slab, the next step is to frame the floor. The framing crew places a huge beam down the center of the house. Boards called joists are placed and then nailed end to end. Joists meet at the center beam. This forms the floor frame. Once the frame is in place, the crew lays plywood on top of the frame. This is called subflooring.

Raising the Walls

When the floor is complete, the framing crew builds and raises the walls. First, though, they must build wall frames. Wall frames are built with two top plates and a bottom plate. Plates are boards at the top and bottom of the walls. The boards between these plates are called studs. Once the wall frames are built, workers raise the frames and nail them to the floor and to each other. Long boards called rafters help to form the ceiling. They are nailed to the top plates. Plywood is sometimes nailed onto these rafters to make an attic floor.

Wall frames are nailed to the floor and to each other to form a room.

Opposite: The framing crew leaves spaces in the walls for windows and doors.
Left: Wooden beams called headers give the walls and roof extra support.

The framing crew must follow the blueprints. The blueprints tell them where to leave spaces for windows or doors. Wooden beams called headers are placed over the areas where windows and doors will be. They give the walls extra strength in those areas. Headers also help to support the roof.

Electricity

Next, electricians and plumbers install wires and pipes. Electricians are in charge of making sure that electricity is able to flow safely throughout a home. An electrician first puts in small metal boxes for outlets, light switches, and light fixtures. Then, he or she runs wires from a central box called a fuse box to the outlets, switches, light fixtures, telephone lines, and cable lines. All the power in the house will be controlled by this fuse box. Wires are attached to power lines outside the home. The local power company must come out to the house to turn on the connection.

Left: An electrician runs wires from a fuse box to the rest of the house.
Opposite above: Air travels throughout the home in ducts that are installed by plumbers.
Opposite: Water moves from room to room inside pipes.

Plumbing

Plumbers install sewer lines, vents, and pipes. Pipes allow water to flow into and out of the home. Sewer lines carry waste outside the home. When you flush the toilet, the contents travel through these lines to a waste treatment plant.

Plumbers install fixtures for sinks, tubs, toilets, and washers. Pipes connect to waterlines underground. They run throughout the home, connecting fixtures. This is how water travels to your sink and shower!

Air ducts are installed for air circulation. Heat or air conditioning travels through vents.

The Roof

Pieces of triangle-shaped wood, called trusses, are used to frame the roof. Trusses sit on top of the walls. The pieces that are used at the front and back of the house are called gable trusses. They are attached to the walls with small metal plates and nails. Trusses are very strong. They distribute weight to the edges of the home so that there is not too much pressure on the roof itself. Once the roof frame is in place, plywood is nailed over the frame to cover the roof.

There are many ways to cover a roof, but the most common way is with shingles. First, the plywood is covered with tar paper. Then, shingles are nailed into the plywood, through the tar paper.

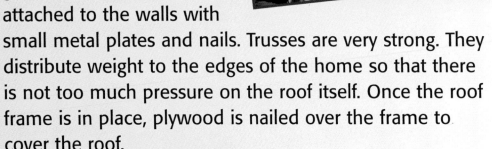

Above: *This roof was specially designed to make the house look unique.*
Opposite: *Black tar paper is nailed to the plywood roof before shingles are attached.*

Colonial and Spanish Style Homes

Houses in America vary in style and design. European immigrants influenced architecture in the United States. The design of homes is different in various parts of the country—so are the materials used to build houses. Spanish style housing was introduced on the West Coast, while English and French designs were popular on the East Coast.

East Coast

Immigrants from England and France brought a style of architecture to the East Coast that is referred to as Colonial style. This type of housing sprang up in New England and stretched down to the southeastern United States with incoming settlers in the 1600s. The size and style of the colonial home varied from state to state, but the basic design was similar.

Colonial style homes are popular in the eastern United States.

These homes were cottages usually built from oak. They had thatched (straw or grass) roofs in the early 1600s. Settlers started to use cedar shingles in the mid-to-late 1600s, though. Cedar shingles did a better job of keeping moisture out of the home. Rainwater and snow would slide off instead of seeping in to the thatched roof.

Colonial homes often had stone chimneys used to ventilate and to let the smoke out from fireplaces and stoves. Rooms called cellars were dug out beneath the cottages. These rooms were kept cool by the ground below and were used to store food.

Most colonial cottages had stone chimneys that helped ventilate the house and let smoke from fireplaces escape.

The design of Spanish style homes like this one is influenced by the architecture of Catholic missions.

West Coast

Spanish colonists constructed mission style homes on the West Coast, especially in California. These homes were made from a concrete-like material called stucco. The Spanish were influenced by Native American homes throughout the Southwest, as well as Mexican and southern Spanish styles. Spanish style homes were designed to be cool in the summer and to heat easily in the sun. This design was made popular by the construction of Catholic missions throughout the West.

In the 1700s, homes were built out of adobe (mud and straw). They were in the shape of a box and usually only one story high. The roof was flat. Adobe homes did not have basements or attics. The homes were built to make use of the sun. The adobe walls kept the inside of the home cool, even as desert temperatures rose up over 100°F (38°C) in the summer. At night, heat from fireplaces and stoves was absorbed by the walls and kept families warm.

Adobe walls kept homes cool during the day and warm at night.

Windows and Doors

Before windows and doors are installed, plastic stripping must be stapled inside their frames. This helps seal the frame and protect the edges of the window or door from the weather. Doors on the inside of the house, between rooms, do not have this plastic stripping.

Doors are installed in wall frames.

Windows are installed in frames that have been carefully measured.

The frames must be carefully measured long before the windows and doors arrive. Once the plastic stripping is in place, the windows and doors are installed. Workers use staples or nails and hinges to set them in place.

Insulation

Insulation is what keeps a home's temperature relatively constant. It keeps heat or cool air in. Insulation comes in big rolls of foam or fiberglass. It is stapled or glued between the studs of a house. Insulation prevents heat or cool air from moving through the walls or ceiling. This keeps energy costs down. It also helps keep the house warm in the winter and cool in the summer.

Insulation helps prevent air from moving through the walls of a house.

Drywall is the last layer of a wall to be put into place before the wall is painted.

Drywall

Putting up drywall makes the inside walls look almost complete before painting. Drywall is made of two thick sheets of paper. Inside the sheets of paper is a material called gypsum. Drywall is heavy and solid. It is screwed or nailed to studs. The edges where drywall sheets meet are joined together using butt joints. Any cracks, dents, or nails are smoothed over with drywall compound. This is called taping.

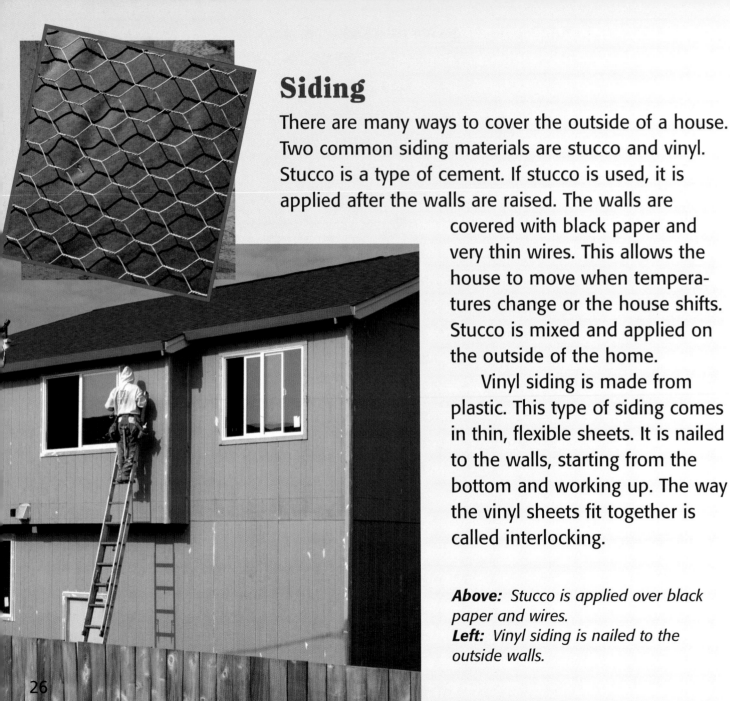

Siding

There are many ways to cover the outside of a house. Two common siding materials are stucco and vinyl. Stucco is a type of cement. If stucco is used, it is applied after the walls are raised. The walls are covered with black paper and very thin wires. This allows the house to move when temperatures change or the house shifts. Stucco is mixed and applied on the outside of the home.

Vinyl siding is made from plastic. This type of siding comes in thin, flexible sheets. It is nailed to the walls, starting from the bottom and working up. The way the vinyl sheets fit together is called interlocking.

Above: *Stucco is applied over black paper and wires.*
Left: *Vinyl siding is nailed to the outside walls.*

Finishing Up

Inside, the subflooring is covered with tar paper or plastic. This prevents moisture from seeping through the floor. Then, particle board is laid down. If the floor is going to be tiled, such as in the bathroom or kitchen, a waterproof layer of "wonder board" is laid down instead of particle board. This is called putting down underlayment.

After the underlayment is down, a subcontractor will put in the furnace. This controls the heat and air conditioning in the home. The furnace is usually located in the basement or inside a closet. Then, the electrician finishes up with the boxes he or she installed earlier. The electrician puts cover plates over the wall outlets and switches.

Above: An electrician puts cover plates over the light switches.
Right: A furnace controls the temperature inside a home.

Cabinets, sinks, and bathtubs are installed during the final stages of construction.

Cabinets are then put in the kitchen and bathroom. They are nailed to the wall studs. Countertops are attached to the top of the cabinets. At this point, the plumber returns to put in the sinks, tubs, faucets, and toilets. He or she will also put in a water heater. A subcontractor must hook up the water lines in the home to the town water and sewer lines outside. This allows water to flow freely to and from the house.

The outside of the house is then painted whatever colors the homeowner chose. When the house is complete, the contractor inspects it. If there are any problems with the construction, he or she makes a list. This is called a punch list. The punch list is given to all of the subcontractors who need to fix things on the house. Once everything is fixed, the house is ready to become a home!

Painting the outside of the house is one of the last steps of construction.

Hearst Castle in San Simeon, California, is the most expensive house ever built. It was built between 1922 and 1939, and sold for $30 million. Today, that is equal to nearly $277 million.

From a House to a Home

Once the homeowner is ready to move in, it's time to paint or wallpaper the inside. It is also time to decorate the home with carpets, curtains, and furniture to make the house feel like a home!

The house is finished and ready for the owner to move in.

Glossary

Architect A person who draws and designs homes

Blueprints The drawings that show the design of the house

Clients People who hire contractors to build their homes

Subcontractors Electricians, plumbers, and construction workers who help build a home

Trusses Triangle-shaped wood

For More Information

Books

Sommer, Robin Langley. *The American House.* San Diego: Thunder Bay Press, 2000.

Website
How Stuff Works: How House Construction Works   www.howstuffworks.com/house.htm

Index